The Story of a Boy Named Will,

by Daniil Kharms

Who Went Sledding Down the Hill

translated by Jamey Gambrell

North-South Books

illustrated by Vladimir Radunsky

Willie went for a sled ride
And slid swiftly down the hillside.
Down the hill he slid his sled,
And hit a hunter as he sped.

Now the hunter,
And Will,
Are sitting on the sled,
Sliding swiftly down the hill.
Down the hill they swiftly sped,
Till they ran into a dog.

Now the dog,
And the hunter,
And the boy named Will,
Are sitting on the sled,
Sliding swiftly down the hill.
Down the hill they swiftly sped,
Till they ran into a fox.

Now the fox,
And the dog,
And the hunter,
And the boy named Will,
Are sitting on the sled,
Sliding swiftly down the hill.
Down the hill they swiftly sped,
Till they ran into a hare.

Now the hare,
And the fox,
And the dog,
And the hunter,
And the boy named Will,
Are sitting on the sled,
Sliding swiftly down the hill.
Down the hill they swiftly sped,
Till they ran into a bear!

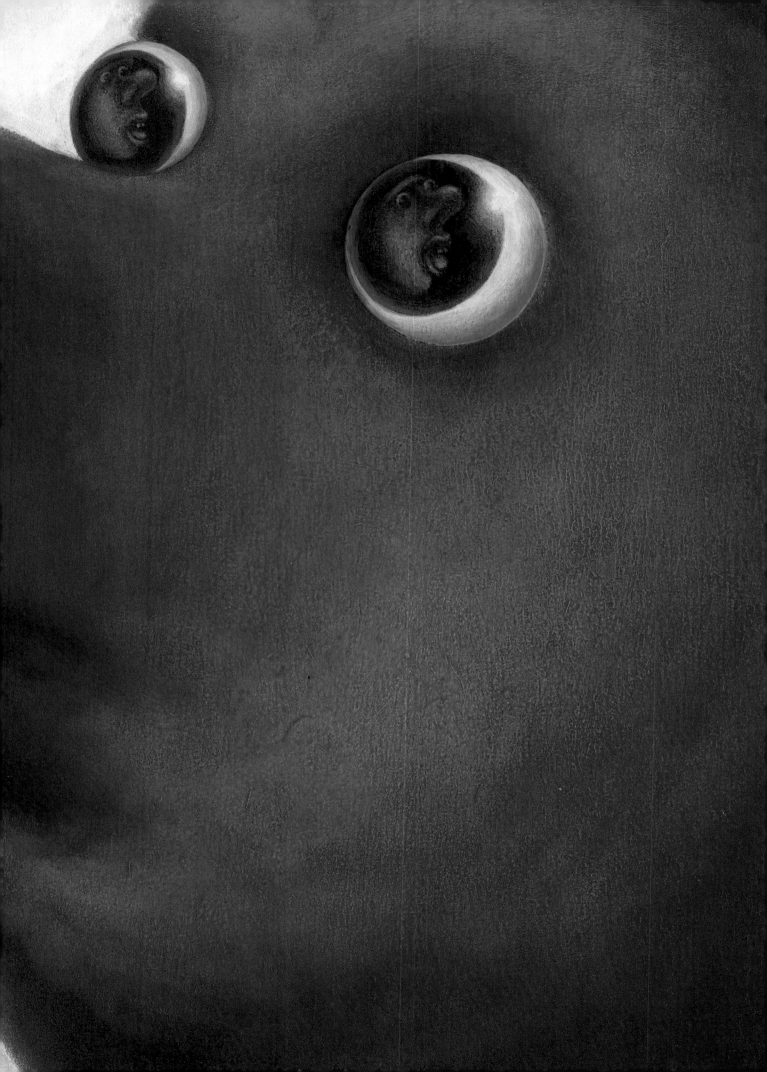

And since then,
I've heard it said,
Willie never
rides his sled.

Translation copyright © 1993 by Jamey Gambrell.
Illustrations copyright © 1993 by Vladimir
Radunsky. All rights reserved. No part of this book
may be reproduced or utilized in any form or by any
means, electronic or mechanical, including photo-
copying, recording, or any information storage and
retrieval system, without permission in writing
from the publisher. Published in the United States
by North-South Books Inc., New York. Published
simultaneously in Great Britain, Canada, Australia,
and New Zealand by North-South Books, an im-
print of Nord-Süd Verlag AG, Gossau Zürich,
Switzerland. Library of Congress Cataloging-in-
Publication Data is available. ISBN 1-55858-214-2
(trade binding) ISBN 1-55858-215-0 (library binding)
A CIP catalogue record for this book is available from
The British Library. ISBN 1-55858-214-2 Designed by
Vladimir Radunsky. Printed in Belgium. The art in
this book was prepared with acrylic and oil paint.
10   9   8   7   6   5   4   3   2   1